# The Very Best Hanukkah Gift

Joanne Rocklin

Illustrated by
Catharine O'Neill

Delacorte Press

Published by
Delacorte Press
a division of Random House, Inc.
1540 Broadway
New York, New York 10036

**Library of Congress Cataloging-in-Publication Data**

Rocklin, Joanne.
    The very best Hanukkah gift / Joanne Rocklin; illustrated by
Catharine O'Neill.
       p.    cm.
    Summary: During his family's eight-day celebration of Hanukkah,
eight-year-old Daniel learns the pleasure of giving and overcomes his
fear of dogs.
    ISBN 0-385-32656-4
    [1. Family life—Fiction.  2. Jews—United States—Fiction.
3. Hanukkah—Fiction.  4. Dogs—Fiction.]  I. O'Neill, Catharine, ill.
II. Title.
PZ7.R59Ve   1999
[Fic]—dc21                            99-10726
                                           CIP

The text of this book is set in 14-point Sabon.
Manufactured in the United States of America
November 1999
10 9 8 7 6 5 4 3
BVG

The
Very Best
Hanukkah
Gift

*For Eric, who also loves stories*
   *—J.R.*

# Contents

# The Very Best Hanukkah Gift

# WEDNESDAY
## Green and Gross

It was the first night of Hanukkah at last. Daniel Bloom felt as if he had been waiting forever. Candlelighting! Stories! Gifts! He raced into the kitchen to see what was for dinner. He knew it would be extra-special. Sure enough, a big platter of pancakes sat on the counter.

"Potato *latkes*! Whoopee!" said Daniel.

But something was wrong. Very wrong. His older brother, Jonah, and little sister,

Amy, were sitting at the kitchen table with grumpy looks on their faces.

"Don't get too excited," Jonah said. "Those *latkes* are really gross."

Mrs. Bloom bent down to check on the chicken roasting in the oven. "They are not gross. You haven't even tasted them yet."

"I don't have to taste them," said Jonah. "You know why? They're green! Who ever heard of green *latkes*?"

Daniel was shocked. "Green?" he asked. "What do you mean?"

He took a closer look. Jonah was right. The *latkes* had little green flecks in them.

"Mommy got the *latkes* at the zoo. They're zoo-cchini!" said Amy, tossing her red curls and giggling at her own joke.

"Excuse me, zucchini *latkes* are nothing to laugh about," Jonah said. "Zucchini *latkes* are sad. Very sad."

"Mom!" cried Daniel. "It's not really Hanukkah without potato *latkes*!"

"Don't worry. It's really Hanukkah,"

said his mother. "I just thought it would be fun to try something different. I think you'll like these." She covered the platter with foil and put it in the top oven to warm. "Now, all of you, please set the table."

"At least we're having chocolate cupcakes for dessert," grumbled Jonah.

"Green and gross! Gross and green! Weirdest *latkes* I've ever seen!" sang Daniel as he put down the silverware at each setting on the dining room table.

Nothing else seemed to be different this Hanukkah, Daniel noticed with relief.

There was the same blue-and-white HAPPY HANUKKAH sign looped across the doorway to the living room. Although this year a torn leg of one *K* dangled forlornly. He would tape it later.

On a table in the living room was the large, freshly polished family menorah. Beside it were Daniel's and Jonah's smaller menorahs, which their parents had bought when they each turned five. All set to light, Daniel noted with satisfaction. Each menorah held one candle on the far right and the *shammes* candle, which was used to light the other candles, in the center space.

And there, in a corner of the dining room, was the big pile of wrapped gifts from his parents, grandparents, and brother and sister. One for each night of Hanukkah for each kid. Three kids. Eight nights. That was—

"There are twenty-two gifts," said Jonah, as if he were reading Daniel's mind. "There should be twenty-four. *Someone*'s gifts aren't out there yet."

"I know *that*," Daniel said. Or he probably *would* have got the math right, if Jonah hadn't interrupted his calculations. Sometimes Jonah thought he knew everything just because he was ten, two whole years older than Daniel.

"And don't worry," said Daniel guiltily. "My gifts for you and Amy will be ready very soon. I'm still working on them."

Daniel eyed the gift pile carefully. One of the packages was probably the Space Explorer CD-ROM he wanted. Probably that flat, square one!

"Green and gross, gross and green!" sang Daniel cheerfully, laying down the napkins.

Mr. Bloom came into the room, carrying another small menorah.

"Whose menorah is that?" asked Daniel.

"It's Amy's. She can light her own this year too," said Mr. Bloom.

"She *can*?" asked Daniel, surprised.

"I'm five now, don't forget!" said Amy, running over. "I'm growing up, up, up!" She carefully placed her menorah on the table beside her older brothers'.

*How come Amy seems to be getting older so quickly?* Daniel thought. He himself felt stuck at being eight years old forever. He went over to the table and picked up his own menorah. With his fingernail he scraped off an old piece of melted wax left over from last year's candlelighting. Last year seemed long ago, but nothing much had changed. He still wasn't so hot at math, for instance. Jonah still beat him at arm wrestling. But he could crack his knuckles now, Daniel reminded himself. And his feet had grown one whole shoe size.

But last year he wasn't afraid of dogs. This year he was, ever since that mean dog bit him in the park last summer. And now there was the big new dog that had just moved into the apartment next door! Daniel shivered. He would try not to think about dogs. Not tonight.

Amy was growing up, but sometimes Daniel felt as if he were sort of growing *down*.

Jonah ran to the window. "It's dusk," he said. "Can we light the candles now?"

"Yes, it's time to begin," said Mrs. Bloom.

Everyone crowded around as Mr. and Mrs. Bloom helped the children light their *shammes* candles. They all chanted the blessings together, beginning with

> *"Barukh atah Adonai*
> *Eloheinu melekh ha-olam*

*Asher kidshanu b'mitzvotav*
*V'tzivanu*
*L'hadlik ner shel Hanukkah."*

Then, with the *shammes* candles, the first night's candles were lit. The flames danced and the menorahs sparkled.

*I feel like I'm in an enchanted room,* thought Daniel. Everything looked different in the soft candlelight. Wouldn't it be great if they could light the Hanukkah candles every single night of the year? Of course, then the candles wouldn't be special. They would be as ordinary as the rug on the floor, which he hardly ever noticed.

Mr. and Mrs. Bloom sat down on the sofa to begin the storytelling. "Thousands of years ago . . . ," said Mrs. Bloom as Amy snuggled beside her.

Daniel and Jonah lay down comfortably on the rug. Daniel loved listening to all his parents' stories, but the story of Hanukkah was one of his favorites.

". . . mean Antiochus, King of the Syrians, ruled the Jewish people of ancient Israel," continued his mother. "The Jews worshiped their own God. They had their own customs, language, and temples."

"Antiochus didn't like that one bit," said Mr. Bloom. "Nosiree. He wanted everyone in his kingdom to think and act and believe exactly the same way."

"Bo-ring," said Daniel from down on the floor.

"Right," said Mr. Bloom. "But Antiochus thought it would be easier to rule if everyone had the same customs and beliefs. He ordered the Jews to burn their holy books and stop observing their religious laws. And he killed those who didn't obey."

"I would run away!" said Amy with a frown. She moved closer to her father on the sofa. "I would run away and hide and never come out."

Daniel smiled to himself. Amy was only five. She didn't remember that the best part of the story was coming.

"Some of the Jews *did* hide, but they had a plan," said Mrs. Bloom. "One brave man, Mattathias, fled to the mountains and caves with his five sons. They organized an army. When Mattathias died, his son Judah took over as leader. Judah's nickname was Maccabee, which means 'hammer' in Hebrew. That's why all of Judah's men were called Maccabees."

"Okay, here comes the part about the elephants," said Daniel.

"Elephants!" exclaimed Amy. "What elephants?"

"Shhh!" said Jonah.

"Antiochus's army was huge," said Mr. Bloom. "His soldiers had fancy weapons, and yes, they had elephants. Thirty-two of them, which marched into battle too. But Antiochus and his elephants didn't stand a chance against that little band of fearless Maccabees, nosiree!"

Daniel closed his eyes. He imagined the noisy, scary battle scenes. How wonderful to be so fearless!

And finally came the part of the story that sent shivers up and down Daniel's spine.

"Well, when the victorious Maccabees returned to their temple, they found it in ruins," said Mrs. Bloom.

"Smashed, bashed, and totally trashed by their enemies," said Mr. Bloom. "Dirt and ashes were everywhere."

*Shiver.*

"So they cleaned everything up and built a new altar," said Mrs. Bloom. "They searched and found only one tiny vial of holy oil to light the temple's menorah."

*Shiver, shiver.*

"It was only enough oil for one day. But—"

"The oil burned for eight days," Daniel couldn't help interrupting his mother. "A miracle!"

"And that's why we celebrate the holiday for eight days," said Mr. Bloom. Then he held up one of the gold-foil–wrapped chocolate coins from the bowl on the coffee table. "The Maccabees threw away all their gold coins with nasty Antiochus's face on them. They put Judah Maccabee's image on their own coins. And that's why we sometimes give money, called *gelt,* at Hanukkah. Or chocolate *gelt,* like these. And of course we exchange other gifts, too."

Daniel glanced at the gift pile. Which gift would he open first? He could hardly wait. His stomach rumbled. He could probably eat that whole bowl of chocolate coins all by himself!

"And to remember the miracle of the oil, we light candles," said his mother. "And we eat fried foods, like *latkes.* Even zucchini *latkes,*" she said with a grin.

Daniel's stomach rumbled again. He could even eat one of those green things, that was how hungry he was!

Jonah shook his head skeptically. "Well, I'm sorry, but I'm older and wiser now. I just don't believe it," he said.

"What do you mean?" asked Daniel, sitting up and staring at his brother.

"Maybe the oil had been lying around in

the sun and it got sort of concentrated or something. Maybe it lasted because of chemistry," said Jonah. "Nobody knew anything about science in those olden times. It wasn't a miracle at all."

Daniel wondered if anyone else had ever had that thought before. True, Jonah had his own chemistry set, a Hanukkah gift from last year. But was Jonah *that* smart? Smarter than Rabbi Feldman? Daniel liked the story much better the old way. He decided that nobody was going to change it.

"Maybe it was a miracle just because it *happened*," he said. "They found the oil just when they needed it. So what if it was chemistry?"

"Science and miracles," said Mr. Bloom, smiling at his sons. "Maybe both at the same time?"

Jonah looked thoughtful. "Maybe," he said.

"Okay, open your presents now. Then let's eat!" said Mrs. Bloom.

Amy got a doll and Jonah a book. Daniel

decided to save the flat, square box for another night, since he sort of knew what it was. He chose to unwrap an intriguingly long, skinny one.

Socks, from his Grandma Fritzie in Florida. *Oh, well,* Daniel thought. There were seven more nights to come.

"See if your new socks fit," said his mother.

Daniel tried them on. "They fit fine," he said.

At dinner Daniel stared at the green-flecked zucchini *latke* beside the chicken leg on his plate. Curious, he took a bite of the *latke,* chewing slowly.

"Not bad!" he said, surprised. "Actually, delicious."

"Not bad at all," said Jonah, his mouth full.

"Another miracle," said their mother.

Soon only one zucchini *latke* was left on the platter.

"It belongs to Daniel," said Jonah, who had been keeping track.

"I'm leaving room for dessert," said Daniel, leaning back contentedly in his chair. "I think I'll have the *latke* as an after-school snack tomorrow." And he wrapped it in his napkin.

After dinner there would be a treasure hunt for chocolate Hanukkah *gelt,* just like every year. Daniel wriggled his feet in his soft new socks. He watched the candles grow smaller and smaller, still flickering merrily.

Zucchini or potato *latkes*—it didn't matter at all. It was really Hanukkah.

# THURSDAY
## That Dog

*Crunch. Crunch.*

Daniel's boots made crunching noises on the snow-packed sidewalk.

He knew there would be one thousand and fifty-five crunches if he took the short-cut home. And two thousand and seventy crunches if he took the long way. But no matter which way he took, short or long, no matter how many crunches, he still had to get there.

And face that dog next door. That *huge*

dog next door. Daniel hadn't actually seen it yet, but he could tell by its bark that the dog was enormous.

*Crunch. Crunch.* Daniel decided to take the long way home, through the park.

"Pretend you're a Maccabee soldier," his older brother, Jonah, had advised him the night before. "I bet that will help build up your courage."

"How do I do that?" Daniel had asked.

"You could recite that poem from *The Happy Hanukkah Holiday Book.*"

"Which poem?"

"I can't believe you forgot it," Jonah had said. "We read it every year."

"Well, I did forget it," Daniel had answered. "A year is a long time."

Jonah himself hardly forgot anything. Squaring his shoulders, he had waved and thrust with an imaginary sword.

> *"I am a Maccabee.*
> *Brave and tall,*

*I fight for freedom*
*For us all!"*

Then Jonah had jumped onto Daniel's bed and waved his pretend sword under Daniel's nose.

*"Maccabees, hey!"*

Wave.

*"Maccabees, ho!"*

Wave.

*"Maccabees, Maccabees,*
*Here we go!"*

Wave, wave.

"Okay, okay, I get the idea," Daniel had said.

Daniel had looked at the pictures in *The*

*Happy Hanukkah Holiday Book*. Then he had read the Maccabee poem a couple of times before turning off the light. To build up his courage, just in case Jonah was right.

*Crunch. Crunch.*

But he wasn't a Maccabee.

Maccabees were tall, muscled men with beards, Jewish soldiers who had lived long ago. They wore white outfits that looked like skirts and carried swords to fight their enemies. They were brave and strong.

He, on the other hand, was an eight-year-old boy on his way home from school in modern times. Wearing a faded ski jacket that used to belong to his brother. He didn't have a sword. He didn't have big muscles. And he wasn't brave, that was for sure.

Daniel's breath met the cold air in thin white puffs.

"I am a dragon, breathing smoke and fire!" Daniel growled.

He imagined himself with pointy yellow

teeth and giant claws. With his long, scaly tail, Daniel the Dragon would snatch up that huge dog. The dog would squirm and struggle to get free.

"No mercy for you! *Aargh!*" Daniel would roar.

And swallow the dog in one slurpy gulp. *Crunch. Crunch.*

But he wasn't a dragon, either.

Daniel had reached the park. He flopped down into a snowbank. He made a few snow angels, then sat up and looked around sheepishly. Had anyone seen him? He hoped not. Making angels in the snow was babyish. Fun, though. Were things more fun back when he was a baby? Or even when he was a little kid, like his sister, Amy?

Sometimes it seemed like it. But sometimes he still felt like a baby, at least where dogs were concerned.

Daniel sighed. He brushed the snow off his jacket. He had to go home sometime.

Tonight was the second night of Hanukkah. They would light the candles and open gifts, and this time there would be potato *latkes* for dinner.

He had to admit that last night's zucchini *latkes* hadn't been so bad. Daniel took his leftover zucchini *latke* from his backpack. He took a big bite of it. That made him feel much better. He put the rest into his pocket and headed home.

*Crunch. Crunch.*

Mr. Rumper, the super, was shoveling snow from the front walk of Daniel's apartment building.

"Lots of snow expected this week, David," said Mr. Rumper, who never seemed to remember Daniel's name.

Daniel took his key from his pocket and trudged slowly up the walk. He unlocked the big front door of the apartment building.

Lately he heard the barking and growling even before he got off the elevator at the second floor. Daniel listened. Nothing. Maybe they weren't home! He started down the hallway.

But today the door of the new tenants' apartment was wide open! Daniel's heart began to hammer. The palms of his hands began to sweat. And then he remembered. Dogs can smell fear.

Daniel took a deep breath. *Calm down,* he told himself. *Walk slowly and quietly. Try, try, try not to smell like fear.*

But there, right in front of him, was that dog!

Daniel stopped walking. He felt as if he had stopped breathing, too.

The dog began lumbering toward him, a huge reddish brown blur. *Thump, thump.* Its feet thumped the floor loudly. Soon the dog would be so close Daniel would see the drool at the side of its mouth. Then he would see its fangs and long, pimply tongue and feel its hot, sour breath. And then he would feel the bite. It was happening all over again!

Daniel froze like a statue. He wanted to run, but his arms and legs just weren't working.

The dog barked hoarsely.

"Rusty? Let me put on your leash," a voice called from inside the apartment.

The dog turned toward the voice, then back to Daniel. Its big, dark eyes met Daniel's in a threatening gaze. Daniel's heart pounded. Then, just as the dog started to come closer, Daniel smelled something.

It was something familiar and wonderful, wafting toward him from his own apartment next door. That smell made him remember what Jonah had told him. It made him remember what he had in his pocket.

*"Maccabees, hey!"* yelled Daniel as loudly and fiercely as he could. And he threw his zucchini *latke* right at the dog.

"Grr-ump?" went Rusty, sniffing at the pancake.

Daniel backed away slowly. Then he quickly turned and raced toward the smell of those potato *latkes* and home.

# FRIDAY
## Daniel's Maccabee

Early the next morning Daniel had a
dream.

It was a hot summer day at the park.
Daniel-in-the-dream ran to the water fountain. He was so thirsty! To his surprise, a
sign said DOGS ONLY. STAY AWAY.

"Some joke!" said Daniel.

He leaned over to take a drink. A dog
was lying beneath the fountain. Daniel bent
down to pet it. Too late, he remembered he
should never pet strange dogs. And this was

the strangest dog he'd ever seen! Its fur was zucchini green and it had little orange ears. Its eyes flashed fire.

Suddenly the dog growled, as if to say, "This is *dog* territory!" It lunged at Daniel's ankle. Its yellow fangs glinted in the sunlight.

"Go away!" Daniel yelled when he felt the bite. He shook his leg as hard as he could. The dog raced away.

And then Daniel woke up. His head hurt and his mouth was dry. He got out of bed and dressed slowly for school, thinking about his scary dream.

"You were hollering in your sleep again," Jonah told him at breakfast.

"I was?" Daniel asked. "What did I say?"

"You said, 'Go away!' and then, 'Grumble, mumble, grumble.' I couldn't really understand you."

"Daniel has bad dreams, Veronica," Amy explained in a loud whisper to her new doll.

"Oh, honey, was it that dream about the dog again?" asked his mother.

"Yes," said Daniel. "Everything was just like it happened in real life."

Well, almost. The dog that bit him last summer hadn't been green like a zucchini, with little orange ears.

"Daniel's afraid of dogs, Veronica," whispered Amy to her doll. "A bad dog bit him last summer at the park. After that, he was afraid to go outside. Sometimes he didn't even want to go to school."

"Cut that out!" said Daniel. "You don't have to tell her *everything*!"

"Yes, I do," Amy said. "Veronica's new around here."

"She's only a *doll*, guys!" said Jonah, laughing.

"I don't care," said Daniel, even though he knew Jonah was right.

Daniel's mother and father looked at each other. Daniel understood that look. It was their "worried about Daniel" look. Lately they acted as if Daniel, not Amy, was the youngest child in the family.

"Did I ever tell you what used to scare me when I was a kid?" asked his father.

Ordinarily Daniel loved his father's "did I ever tell you" stories. But this morning Daniel was grumpy. And his head was pounding.

"Probably," he said.

"You never told *me*," said Jonah.

Mr. Bloom carefully buttered a piece of toast. "You may not believe this. Promise not to laugh?"

"*We* promise!" said Amy, waving Veronica.

Daniel shrugged.

Mr. Bloom bit into his toast and chewed. "I used to be afraid of clowns," he said finally.

"*Clowns?*" asked Daniel incredulously.

"A clown bit you?" asked Amy.

Daniel and Jonah laughed. Now Daniel felt like Amy's big brother again.

"No, a clown never bit me," said Mr.

Bloom. "But it was a clown who lit the match just before the Great Alphonso was shot out of the cannon at the circus. I was six years old. What a noise that cannon made! And there was poor Al, flying from one end of the circus tent to the other! I almost fell out of my seat. After that, I could never look at a clown without shaking. And they *are* kind of scary looking, you have to admit."

"So then what happened?" asked Daniel, picking at his cereal. His throat felt scratchy.

Mr. Bloom thought for a moment. "Well, I guess I just grew out of it."

"But how?" Daniel asked.

His father looked stumped and took another bite of his toast. Daniel was surprised. Usually his dad had an answer for everything.

"I'm not sure how I did it, kiddo," Mr. Bloom said gently. "I'll try to remember."

Daniel put his head down on the table. "I'm not feeling very well," he said.

"Really?" asked Mrs. Bloom.

"Really," said Daniel. "I promise I'm not faking."

His mother put a cool hand on his forehead. "Oh," she said. "You do feel warm."

She brought Daniel the thermometer. He kept it in his mouth for three minutes by the kitchen clock.

"Ninety-nine point nine," said Jonah, reading the thermometer over his mother's shoulder. "One point three degrees above normal."

Mrs. Bloom looked worried. "I have that big meeting today," she said. "I really have to go to work."

"No problem," said Mr. Bloom. "Daniel and I will stay home together. I have some phone calls I can make from here."

Jonah looked at Daniel enviously. "You get to try out your new Space Explorer CD-ROM!" he said.

But Daniel didn't really feel like playing with his Hanukkah present. When his mother had left for work, and his brother and sister for school, he lay down on the living room couch.

"I'll be on the phone in the kitchen if you need me," said his father.

"Okay," said Daniel. He closed his eyes. He listened to the gentle murmuring of his father on the telephone. He could hear the honking drone of the traffic outside.

Pretty soon he heard the marching of elephants.

*Thump. Thump. Thump.*

Elephants? Daniel-in-the-dream sat up. A tired-looking man in a white outfit was drinking at that same water fountain in the park.

"You're a Maccabee!" said Daniel.

The man stopped drinking. "I sure am," he said, looking surprised. He wiped his mouth with the back of his sunburned hand. "But how did you know?"

"Oh, I've seen drawings of you guys in books," Daniel said. "I'm Daniel."

Daniel and the Maccabee shook hands. "We still tell your story," Daniel said.

"How fearless and brave you were, and everything."

The Maccabee straightened his shoulders proudly. "We were brave, all right! But fearless? Are you kidding?" He gave a little snort. "Do you think I spend my day singing 'Maccabees, ho!'? Nosiree! Listen, David—"

"Daniel."

"Daniel," said the Maccabee. He did two quick push-ups, then patted the ground beside him. "Have a seat. I'll tell you a story."

"I like stories," said Daniel, sitting down.

The Maccabee leaned comfortably against the water fountain.

"When the fighting began," he said, "at first I hid in a cave with my brother and sisters. We were afraid to go out. But inside the cave it was dark and cold. We missed the rest of our family, our temple, and the sky. So one day I said to my brother, Jonah, and my sisters, Amy and Veronica—"

"Hey, those are the same—" interrupted Daniel.

"I said, 'No more hiding! We must fight for our people's freedom!' " The Maccabee waved his fist in the air.

*Thump. Thump. Thump.*

"Oh, no! Antiochus's elephants!" cried the Maccabee, jumping up. He had a scared look on his face. "I've got to join the others now."

"Good luck," said Daniel. Then he remembered something. "Hey, elephants love peanuts! Try giving them some! Peanuts!"

But the Maccabee was far away, a small speck running toward the hills.

"What's this about peanuts?" asked Mr. Bloom, putting his hand on Daniel's forehead. "Were you dreaming about the circus?"

"Not exactly," Daniel said.

*Good thing it was just a dream,* he thought. He had given the Maccabee terrible advice. If the elephants knew that the soldier had peanuts, they'd come charging right at him!

But maybe the Maccabee could hide the

peanuts in the hills. The elephants would run here and there, trying to sniff them out. And then Antiochus's troops would get lost on the way to battle. Daniel hoped he would meet that Maccabee again. Then he could tell him his peanut plan.

"Which reminds me," said Mr. Bloom, sitting down on the couch. "I remember what happened now. My best friend invited me to go to the circus. He could invite only one special friend. It was his birthday and he really wanted me to go. So I decided to keep my eyes closed whenever the clowns came out."

"But the clowns come out all the time," said Daniel.

"True. You could say I didn't really *see* the circus. I kind of listened to it."

Daniel giggled.

"Well, it was a start," said his father.

# SATURDAY
## Big Joe Zucchini

The next day was Saturday. A beautiful Saturday! The sun sparkled on fresh snow. The sky was blue and clear. Daniel could see his friends Sam and Lara building a snowman in the little yard in front of the apartment building. Daniel opened the living room window and leaned out.

"Hey, Daniel," called Sam. "Come help us."

"I'll be right down," said Daniel.

"Not with a fever, you won't!" said Mrs. Bloom, coming into the room.

"But, Mom!" cried Daniel. "My temperature is only ninety-nine degrees, right? Hardly any fever at all. You said so yourself."

Mrs. Bloom closed the window. "It's still a fever," she said firmly. "You want to be well for the family party on Wednesday, don't you?"

"But my throat doesn't hurt anymore. I feel fine. Watch this!" said Daniel. He did two push-ups on the living room floor.

"Excellent. But you still have to stay inside until your temperature is normal," said his mother, leaving the room. "I've got some paperwork to do now. But in a little while I'll challenge you to a game of Monopoly."

Daniel sighed. He looked out the window again. He watched Lara toss a snowball to Sam.

"Good shot," said Daniel, opening the window.

"Coming down?" Sam asked. He began rolling the snowball in the snow to make it bigger.

Daniel shook his head. "I've still got a fever."

"Too bad!" said Sam. He put the big snowball on top of the snowman. "There. That's his head."

"Daniel, I know how you can help us," said Lara. "Our snowman needs a face. Clothes, too."

"Be right back," said Daniel.

He ran to the hall closet. He found a scarf and a football helmet.

"Here," he said, tossing them out the window.

"Great," said Sam. "But he still needs a face."

"Just a minute," said Daniel. He ran into the kitchen. "Mom, where are the carrots?" he asked, peering into the refrigerator bin.

"We're all out," said his mother.

"I'll take this zucchini instead," Daniel said.

"But, Daniel," said Mrs. Bloom, "a *raw* zucchini? How about snacking on an apple?"

"A zucchini is exactly what I want," Daniel said.

In his bedroom Daniel found two gold-foil–wrapped circles of chocolate Hanukkah *gelt*. He found a piece of red yarn. He put everything into a bag. Then he ran back to the living room window.

"Here, guys, catch!" he called.

"Perfect," said Sam. He put the gold circles, the yarn, and the zucchini in the right places. "Our snowman is finished."

Lara and Sam began tossing snowballs at each other.

"Hey, let's all play football!" said Daniel. "Let's pretend the snowman is Big Joe Zucchini, the best quarterback in the league."

Lara and Sam huddled around Big Joe, who told them what to do. Daniel leaned out the window to hear the play too.

"Okay," said Lara. "Pretend I just got the ball from Joe!"

"I'm in the end zone," said Daniel. "Throw the ball to me!"

Lara threw the snowball to Daniel, hard and fast. The crowd went wild!

"I've got it! I've got it!" yelled Daniel.

But he was wrong. The snowball sailed through the window. *Splat!* It hit a lampshade, then dribbled onto the rug.

"What's going on in here?" asked Mrs. Bloom, running into the room.

"A football game," said Daniel sheepishly, straightening the lampshade.

"Oh, Daniel," said Mrs. Bloom.

Daniel ran to the kitchen. He returned with some paper towels to clean up the mess. His mother felt his forehead. "You'll get even sicker if you don't rest up," she said, closing the window.

Resting up was Boring with a capital *B*, thought Daniel. He looked out the window. Only Big Joe Zucchini remained outside. Sam and Lara had gone home. Boring. Boring. Boring.

Daniel opened the window again and

leaned out. "Hey, Zucchini! What's up?" he asked.

He remembered a ventriloquist he had seen on TV. The ventriloquist could throw his voice anywhere. Maybe he could do that too. Daniel closed his eyes and concentrated hard.

*"I'm Bored with a capital B,"* said the snowman in a squeaky voice.

Mr. Bloom and Amy were coming up the walk. Amy was carrying her doll, Veronica. Quickly Daniel ducked down below the windowsill.

*"That doll sure is funny looking,"* said Big Joe Zucchini.

"She is not! Who said that?" Amy asked.

*"Over here! The guy in the football helmet,"* said the snowman. *"They call me Big Joe Zucchini."*

"Snowmen can't talk," said Amy. "Anyway, you sound like my brother Daniel."

Daniel heard his father chuckle. And then he heard something else.

Barking. Ferocious barking.

Daniel peeked above the windowsill. That huge dog, Rusty, and a young woman were coming up the walk. The young woman almost dropped her bag of groceries as Rusty strained at his leash. He was barking loudly at Big Joe Zucchini.

"Quiet, Rusty!" said the dog's owner. Rusty stopped barking. But he glared fiercely at the snowman, growling every now and then.

*That dog is a big bully,* thought Daniel, who was now glad to be inside. He ducked down beneath the windowsill again.

"Sorry about the barking," the young woman was saying. "Rusty loves green vegetables. He thinks the nose on that snowman should be *his* to eat. I'm Jane. Rusty and I just moved in. We live on the second floor."

"We live on the second floor too! We're neighbors!" cried Amy happily.

*Who cares?* thought Daniel unhappily.

"I'm Mark Bloom," said Mr. Bloom. "This is Amy."

"This is Veronica," said Amy. "And that's Big Joe Zucchini. If he talks, it's really my brother Daniel hiding behind that window up there."

Neither Daniel nor the snowman introduced himself personally.

"Daniel must be the boy I heard having a conversation with Rusty the other day," Jane said. "I've been wanting to meet him."

"Daniel?" asked Mr. Bloom in a surprised voice.

"He fed something to Rusty that Rusty just loved. My dog's been searching for Daniel all over the second floor," said Jane.

"It couldn't have been Daniel," said Amy. "It was probably my other brother, Jonah."

"*It was Daniel,*" said the snowman. "*He fed that dog a zucchini latke.*"

Jane laughed. "Well," she said, "Rusty ate it all up. Didn't you, Rusty?"

Daniel peeked out the window again. Rusty had rolled over onto his back. Jane was tickling his big stomach.

"Veronica and I like dogs," said Amy. She tickled the dog's stomach too. "He's so cute!"

Daniel could see Rusty's long yellow teeth. Cute? *Cute?*

"Well, I've got to go home now and start my Christmas baking," said Jane.

"Do you leave out cookies for Santa?" asked Amy. "My friend Samantha does that."

"Yes. And the cookies are always gone in the morning," said Jane with a wink.

"Really!" exclaimed Amy. "Does Santa eat them?"

*"Are you kidding? That* dog *eats them,"* said Big Joe Zucchini.

Amy frowned at the snowman. "How do you know? It *could* be Santa!"

"Would you kids like to come by Tuesday, Christmas Eve, for some cookies and hot chocolate?" asked Jane. "Around seven-thirty? Rusty will show you all the neat tricks he knows."

"Jonah and I will come," Amy said. "But Daniel won't. He's afraid of dogs. He's a baby that way."

"*He is not!*" said Big Joe Zucchini. "*I bet he'll be there.*"

*Oh, no! Why did you have to say* that, *Joe?* thought Daniel.

# SUNDAY
## The Secret Present

On the fifth night of Hanukkah, Daniel received a yellow glow-in-the-dark marker pen from Jonah. He decided to use the pen to work on the gifts he was making for his family.

First Daniel cut out four big circles. Then he colored the circles with his yellow marker pen to look like Hanukkah *gelt*.

On the first circle he wrote:

Happy HANUKKAH,
Jonah Bloom!
You're a lucky guy!
I, your brother,
Daniel Bloom, will make
your bed every Monday
morning for one
month.

Daniel decorated the circle with menorah and *dreidel* stickers. He leaned back and looked with satisfaction at what he had written. Jonah hated making his bed. He would be pleased.

Next, Amy. Daniel thought for several minutes. Finally on the second circle he wrote:

read

2 U on days.

Daniel frowned. Amy's gift wasn't as good as Jonah's, he realized. Daniel usually read to Amy whenever she asked, no matter what day of the week it was. Maybe he'd come up with something better later, he thought guiltily. He still had time.

Next, his parents.

"It isn't necessary to get us Hanukkah gifts," his parents always said.

But Daniel thought it was fun to give his parents gifts. It made him feel grown up. The gifts had to be homemade, or cost less than two dollars. Those were his parents' rules. Daniel had thought about their gifts for a long time. And his father's gift was terrific, if he did say so himself.

From under his bed, Daniel pulled out a
long, skinny box of plastic wrap. He
wrapped the box with Hanukkah gift paper. Then he made the card on one of his
big yellow circles. He wrote:

Dear Dad,
   Every time you trim
your mustache, put some
of this over the soap
first. Then Mom won't
get mad at you for
getting hairs on the soap.
HAPPY HANUKKAH!
        Love,
        Your son Daniel

Only his mother's gift was left. Daniel took a shoe box from under his bed and opened it. Inside the shoebox was a little painted piece of clay.

"What's that?" asked Jonah, wandering into the bedroom.

"Mom's gift," Daniel said.

Jonah leaned over and looked into the shoe box. "Interesting. But what is it?" he asked.

"It's a secret," said Daniel.

Actually, the present was so secret, he wasn't even sure what it was himself. It had started off as a little jewelry box when he had first shaped the clay at school. But when he'd dried it in the school kiln, one side had curled like a leaf, and the other side had flattened out. It wouldn't hold much jewelry, but he had painted it blue and white anyway. His father had told him it was a nice piece of modern art.

"Come on, tell me what it is," said Jonah.

"I told you. It's a secret," Daniel said.

Jonah leaped on Daniel. The boys rolled

on the floor. Jonah pinned Daniel's arms down.

"One more chance! Tell me?" asked Jonah.

"No way," yelled Daniel.

"Then I'll show no mercy," shouted Jonah. "You are to be tickled to death!"

Daniel pushed as hard as he could and, to his surprise, broke free. He had never been able to do *that* before. Maybe his muscles *were* getting stronger!

"What's going on in there?" called Mrs. Bloom from the kitchen.

"Nothing," said Jonah.

"Nothing," said Daniel.

"Aw, who cares what your secret present is?" said Jonah, flopping down on his bed with a book.

Daniel sighed. He cared, that was who. How can you give someone a gift when you're not sure what it is yourself? He wrapped his mother's gift anyway, decorating the package with the rest of his Hanukkah stickers. Then he went into the kitchen, where his parents were baking cookies.

"Mom, I just want to warn you," Daniel said. He paused to pop a menorah cookie into his mouth.

"Warn me about what?" asked Mrs. Bloom. She sprinkled blue and white sugar on a tray of unbaked Stars of David.

"Well," said Daniel, swallowing the last bit of cookie, "you may not think the Hanukkah present I made you is so great."

"Of course I will! It's the thought that counts, honey. You know that," said his mother. Then she put her hands on Daniel's shoulders and looked into his eyes. "I will cherish your gift always," she said.

"I hope so," Daniel said gloomily.

"Hey," said Mr. Bloom, "did I ever tell you the story about me and the potato chips?"

"No," said Daniel, perking up. He sat down at the kitchen table. Today he was in the mood to hear one of his father's stories.

Mr. Bloom poured himself a cup of coffee, then sat down beside Daniel. "When I was about your age, I loved potato chips. Still do, as you know. I got it into my head to write a thank-you note to the potato chip company for the wonderful potato chips they produced. I wrote the letter in my best handwriting and mailed it off."

Daniel liked to imagine his father as a young boy. In old photos, with no mustache, he looked sort of like Daniel.

"About a month after I wrote that letter," continued his father, "a big van pulled up to my apartment building. I happened to be looking out the window. And a driver hopped out carrying a great big can of . . . ?"

"Wow! Potato chips?"

"You guessed it. They really liked my letter. So after I ate the potato chips—took me about a week—I sat down and wrote a poem about my favorite chocolate bar. Sent that off to the chocolate bar company."

"And you got some chocolate bars?" asked Daniel.

"Half a dozen. Ate them, then sat down and wrote a letter about my favorite soda pop, and you know the rest."

"You got sodas!" said Daniel, giggling.

"Right. Then I had this brilliant idea. You see, my parents' car was in terrible shape. It needed a new carburetor and a paint job. Even its dents had dents! So I wrote a long letter to the president of the automobile company, praising his wonderful cars. And then I waited."

Mr. Bloom paused to sip his coffee.

"And?" asked Daniel impatiently.

"I waited. And I waited. Every morning I looked up and down the street, expecting to see one of those long trailers carrying my parents' shiny new car. It was this very time of year, I remember, and I figured it would make a terrific Hanukkah gift. Probably the best gift they'd ever received in their lives! And then it came."

"Wow!" said Daniel. "A car!"

"Well, no. A note from a big-shot executive at the company, thanking me for my interest in their cars. I was so disappointed, I cried. I had really believed the car would come."

Daniel nodded. He would have cried too.

"I showed the big shot's letter to my father and told him the whole story. He said the car wasn't important. He said it was the thought that counted. Of course I didn't believe him."

Mr. Bloom put his arm around Daniel. "But now I do," he said. "I really do."

"A gift of love," said Mrs. Bloom. "That's the very best gift of all."

Daniel was quiet for a few moments. "It would have been nice to get that car, though," he said.

"You're right," said Mr. Bloom, who had gone back to cutting out Hanukkah cookies. "It would have been nice."

Daniel went into his bedroom. On the fourth yellow circle he wrote:

Dear Mom,
  This is a thought box.
I made it myself.
There are lots of good
thoughts in it from me to you.
(You can also put your
  ring in this box when
  you take it off.)
HAPPY Hanukkah!
    Love,
      your son
        Daniel

# MONDAY
## Oil, Zoil

Jonah was writing a Hanukkah poem for the big party on Wednesday. He wanted to tell the entire Hanukkah story in rhyme, he said. Daniel knew that took a lot of brain-power.

But there was a secret to rhyming. And Daniel had finally figured it out.

"Maybe you can use an assistant," Daniel said. "A rhyming assistant."

Jonah looked up from his papers. His

cheeks were flushed. His hair stuck out from the sides of his head. He had a pencil behind his ear.

"Well, okay," Jonah said. He reached for a Hanukkah cookie from the plate on his desk. "See what rhymes you come up with for 'oil' and 'miracle.' And also 'Antiochus,' if you have time."

"Easy," said Daniel.

First he got his own plate of Hanukkah cookies. Then he sharpened two pencils. He put one pencil behind his ear. He wrote out the alphabet, all twenty-six letters, just the way Jonah had. And he crossed out the vowels, A, E, I, O, U, also the way Jonah had. Then he wrote oil beside each of the alphabet letters that were left.

"Boil, coil, doil," whispered Daniel. He put a circle around boil and coil. He stopped to eat a cookie. He studied his list. "Is 'doil' a word?" he asked.

"No," said Jonah.

Daniel worked slowly. There was a lot to

think about. He ate two more cookies. Finally he came to *zoil,* but he did not put a circle around it. "Done!" he said proudly. "Well, my first list anyway."

Jonah studied Daniel's list. "You circled 'loil' and 'roil,' " he said.

"Right," said Daniel, munching on another cookie. "The Maccabees were *loil* to one another. Antiochus was a king. He was *roil.*"

Jonah giggled. He took the pencil from behind his ear and wrote *loyal* and *royal.* "You spell them like this."

"Oh," said Daniel.

*Sometimes there's just too much to know!* thought Daniel as he got into bed. Rhyming was harder than he'd thought. He would continue tomorrow.

Jonah climbed into his bed too. " 'Loyal' is a good word for my poem," he said. "Now think of a rhyme for 'miracle.' "

"That's a tough one," said Daniel drowsily. And then he fell asleep.

\* \* \*

*Creak, creak.*

Daniel woke up suddenly. He glanced at the clock on his night table. 11:48 P.M.

*Rustle, rustle.*

What were those noises?

Daniel searched for his special radio, a Hanukkah present from the previous night. Attached to the radio was a handy flashlight for emergencies. He hadn't expected to use it so soon! Quietly he swung his legs over the side of the bed and felt for his slippers with his feet. He switched on the flashlight. Then he tiptoed from his bedroom.

*Rustle, creak.*

Daniel poked his head into the living room. A dark figure was curled up on the floor near the fireplace! Daniel's heart began to thud. A burglar? He was just about to run for his parents when—

*Munch, munch.*

The dark figure was chewing something! It reached toward a plate on the floor. Daniel tiptoed closer. The dark figure turned toward him and jumped up.

It wasn't a burglar at all. It was Amy.

"Who's there?" she demanded.

"It's me, silly. Daniel," Daniel answered in a loud whisper. "What are you doing?"

Amy sighed, picking up the plate from the floor. She flopped down on the couch with her doll, Veronica, on her lap. Daniel sat down too.

"Veronica and I fell asleep waiting for Santa," Amy said. She smelled like cookies.

"Christmas Eve is *tomorrow* night," said Daniel. He switched on the lamp. There were two cookies on the plate, one shaped like a *dreidel,* the other like a Star of David.

"But I wanted Santa to taste our cookies before you and Jonah ate them all up," said Amy. "I thought Santa might be out practicing in the sky tonight."

Daniel pointed to the window. "Look! There he goes!" he cried.

Amy turned her head. Quickly Daniel grabbed the Star of David cookie and hid it behind a pillow.

"Oh, sorry," he said. "It wasn't Santa. It

was a shooting star. But guess what? Santa was here already. You missed him."

"Really?" asked Amy, her eyes wide. "How do you know?"

"How many cookies did you put on the plate?" asked Daniel.

"Four," said Amy.

"How many did *you* eat?" asked Daniel.

"Two," said Amy.

"Two and two makes four, right?" Daniel pointed to the plate. "But look! There's only one cookie left. Santa ate the other one while you were sleeping."

Amy stared at the cookie. "Wow!" she cried. "Santa's probably never had Hanukkah cookies before."

"Oh, I'm sure he has," Daniel said. "Although not as good as ours, of course."

"Maybe I'll stay up again tomorrow night," Amy said.

Daniel smiled to himself. He remembered when he had been Amy's age. He had wanted to meet the real Santa too. But deep down he had always been glad *his* gifts came from his family. *What if Santa lost his way in a snowstorm one year, or a great gust of wind blew all the gifts from his sleigh?* he used to wonder. All of a sudden Daniel felt much, much older and smarter than Amy. It was a good feeling. It was probably how Jonah felt every single minute of his life.

Amy yawned and leaned against Daniel. "You know what, Daniel?" she said.

"What?" Daniel asked.

"One day maybe one of our Hanukkah gifts will be a dog," said Amy. She looked at Daniel. "Right?"

Daniel stared at his feet. He didn't say anything.

"Some dogs are nice," said Amy. "Rusty is."

Daniel shrugged. All of a sudden he didn't feel like such a big brother anymore. He remembered how Amy had hugged Rusty just that morning, when Rusty had been out for his walk with Jane. And how he, Daniel, had scampered inside the apartment building like a scared rabbit.

"Well, I guess I'll go back to bed now," Amy said. "Good night."

"Good night," said Daniel.

*Wouldn't it be great if I could give Amy a dog for Hanukkah?* thought Daniel. One of those tiny puppies with big floppy ears. Amy would be so happy. "This is the best Hanukkah present ever! Thank you, Daniel!" she'd say.

Except that tiny puppies grow up to be big dogs, of course. And it would take a miracle for Daniel to stop being afraid of dogs. Amy was only five. She believed in miracles. But wouldn't it be great if one could really happen?

*Miracle, biracle.*

Not easy to find a rhyme for it, either.

Daniel munched on the Star of David cookie slowly, point by point. Maybe he'd tell Amy that he, not Santa, had eaten the cookie.

And maybe he wouldn't.

# TUESDAY
## The Riddle

On the seventh night of Hanukkah, Daniel chose to open a small box wrapped in white paper with a blue bow. He hadn't really noticed that gift on the other nights. It had been hidden behind a big tin of popcorn he'd unwrapped the night before.

He opened the card first, because that was the polite thing to do. It said:

Dear Daniel,
    Here's a riddle. What is a four-letter word that begins with L? That's what

this gift will bring to you. (It used to belong to your mom.)
Hugs and kisses special delivery from California,
Grandma Ava and Grandpa Rick

Inside the box was a silver *dreidel*. Daniel spun the little top across the living room floor, then read the note to his family.

"I know the answer to that riddle," said Amy. *"L-L-L-Latkes?"*

Daniel looked at Jonah. They both laughed.

"Lunch?" asked Amy.

"It's a *four*-letter word," Jonah said.

"L-L-L-Lion?" asked Amy.

Daniel and Jonah lay down on the floor, snorting with laughter.

Amy looked as if she was going to cry. Suddenly Daniel felt bad. "It's *L-U-C-K*. That spells *luck*," he said.

"A lucky *dreidel*!" said Amy.

Daniel read the names of the Hebrew letters on the dreidel's four sides. *Nun. Gim-*

*mel. He. Shin.* He knew they were the first letters of the words in the sentence *Nes gadol hayah sham,* which means "a great miracle happened there."

That miracle again. A shiver went up and down Daniel's spine. He twirled the *dreidel* once more, staring at the silver blur. What if his new *dreidel* really *was* lucky, just as his grandparents had promised?

"Mom, did this *dreidel* bring you good luck?" Daniel asked.

"Absolutely," said Mrs. Bloom. She spread both arms wide. "Look how lucky I am today."

"Come on, Mom, *really,*" said Daniel.

But his mother just smiled.

"It's just a top for an old Hanukkah game," said Jonah. "It doesn't have special powers or anything."

Mr. Bloom picked up the *dreidel.* It glinted in the light of the Hanukkah candles. "I don't know about that," he said. "This little top and its games were very important in the days of the Maccabees."

"Really?" asked Daniel.

"Story time!" said Amy, plopping down on the couch.

"A short one. Dinner is almost ready," said her father. He sat down on the couch beside Amy. "We already told you how King Antiochus forbade the Jews to study the Jewish Bible. Well, some boys already knew the whole thing by heart."

"The whole thing? Wow!" said Jonah.

"They would get together to study secretly," continued Mr. Bloom. "One of the boys would be chosen as the lookout. 'Soldiers coming!' he would warn. 'Hide those books!' And out would come their spinning tops and other toys. The soldiers would be fooled, thinking the boys were playing games. They didn't guess what those boys were *really* doing!"

Sometimes he himself did just the opposite, thought Daniel guiltily. He pretended to do his homework when he was really playing on the computer.

"Who knows?" said Mr. Bloom. "Maybe

a Jewish soldier, going into battle, would think about those *dreidel* games. He would remember his friends and family at home. And he would feel strong. Maybe he would even feel lucky."

At dinner Daniel placed the *dreidel* near his plate while he ate. Did he actually feel a tingly feeling at the back of his neck? A fluttery feeling in his chest? A lucky feeling all over? Yes! Definitely.

"I challenge you guys to a *dreidel* game!" Daniel said to his sister and brother after dinner.

Jonah looked at his watch. "We said we'd go next door tonight. It's almost seven-thirty. I want to see that dog do tricks."

"Come on, just one game," Daniel begged. "I *do* feel lucky tonight! I know I'll win for sure."

*And maybe,* thought Daniel, *the game will be so much fun they'll forget all about going next door.*

"I'll set the kitchen timer for fifteen minutes," said Jonah. "At the end of that time we'll see who's the winner."

Daniel sighed. Jonah was just too smart for him.

"Come play with us, Amy," said Jonah. "It's more fun with three people."

Jonah brought out the timer and the bowl of chocolate *gelt*. He gave everyone seven pieces. Jonah, Daniel, and Amy sat down on the living room rug.

"Veronica wants to play too," said Amy.

"Dolls can't play!" said Daniel.

"Yes, they can," said Amy, folding her arms across her chest. "I won't play if she can't."

"Oh, let her play," said Jonah. He counted out seven pieces of *gelt* for Veronica, too. "Now I'll review the rules for you dummies who don't know them."

"That's a mean thing to say," said Daniel.

"I'm talking to the doll," said Jonah. "Okay. Everyone put one piece of *gelt* into the middle. That's the pot."

Everyone did that, including Veronica/Amy.

Jonah held up the *dreidel*. "See these Hebrew letters on the sides of the *dreidel*?"

"I see them," said Amy. "So does Veronica. Right, Veronica?"

Daniel rolled his eyes.

"When it's your turn to spin the *dreidel*," continued Jonah, "if it falls on *nun*, just do nothing. If it falls on *gimmel*, take the whole pot. *He*, take half the pot, or half plus one if it's an odd number. *Shin*, give half your own pile. And everyone puts in one piece after each person's turn."

Jonah set the timer for fifteen minutes. "The person who has the most *gelt* when it rings is the winner."

*Tick, tick, tick* went the timer.

Jonah spun the *dreidel*. "*Nun*. Do nothing. Oh, well. Don't forget to put one piece in the pot after each turn, everybody."

Amy spun. *Shin.*

"Give half of your pile to the pot. That's three," Daniel told her.

Veronica/Amy spun. "*He!* Take half!" shouted Amy. Daniel helped her figure out how much that was.

Daniel spun. He wished for luck. "*Gimmel!* Take the whole pot!" he cried. Daniel scooped up all the pieces.

*Tick, tick, tick.*

Soon Jonah, then Amy, had no *gelt* left and were out of the game. Daniel had eight pieces in his pile. Veronica had twelve. There were eight pieces in the pot.

*Tick, tick, tick.* The timer showed two more minutes to play.

"This is a tense moment in Bloom City, folks," said Jonah, whispering into a pretend microphone. "Two *dreidel* masters, Veronica and Daniel, fighting to win. Can Daniel make it back to the top?"

Veronica/Amy spun. *Nun.* Do nothing.

Veronica/Amy and Daniel each put one piece back into the pot.

*Tick, tick, tick.*

Veronica/Amy still had four pieces more than Daniel. Was a *doll* going to beat him?

He spun. *Gimmel* again! Take the whole pot!

"Yes!" Daniel shouted, scooping up the pieces.

Each player put one piece back into the pot.

*Tick, tick, tick.*

"Only half a minute of play left," whispered Jonah. "The pot has two. The score is Daniel, sixteen; Veronica, ten. It's not over yet, folks."

"It sure isn't!" said Amy, spinning the *dreidel* for Veronica.

*He.* Take half. Amy gave her doll one piece from the pot.

*Brr-ing! Brr-ing!* went the timer.

Daniel looked down at his *gelt.* "I won!" he cried. Grandma Ava and Grandpa Rick had been right. He had *L-U-C-K!*

"Phooey," said Amy.

"Veronica put up a good fight," said Jonah, getting up from the floor. "Time to go see that dog."

Amy brightened and jumped up too. "Are

you coming, Daniel?" she asked. "You said you would."

"Yes," said Daniel, suddenly feeling brave as well as lucky. "Of course I'm coming."

Mr. and Mrs. Bloom put down their newspapers and stared. Mr. Bloom grinned.

"Good going, Daniel," said his father. "Now, remember what we always tell you. There are two signs of a friendly dog. The ears will be down. The tail will be wagging like crazy."

Daniel looked at the lucky *dreidel* in his hand. "I'll remember, Dad. Don't worry."

"Here, take these with you for our new neighbor," said Mrs. Bloom. She gave Jonah a platter of Hanukkah cookies.

"Maccabees, hey! Maccabees, ho!" sang Daniel, marching down the hall in front of his brother and sister. "Come on, troops, let's go!"

He could hardly believe it. Here he was, going to meet a dog, and he wasn't even afraid.

Much.

Just a tiny flutter in his stomach, that was all.

Jane opened the door. "Hello!" she said. "Hanukkah cookies! Thank you. I have some cookies for you, too."

Daniel could hear Rusty barking. The tiny flutter in Daniel's stomach had grown as big as an ocean wave. His heart began to pound. His knees felt weak.

"This is Jane, guys," said Amy. "These are my brothers, Jonah and Daniel."

"Hi," said Jane.

Rusty barked again, more loudly this time. Daniel backed away from the door. He felt so ashamed! *What a baby I am, after all,* he thought. "I'm sorry," he said in a small voice. "I'm afraid of dogs. A dog bit me once."

Jane put her hand on his shoulder. "Daniel, I understand," she said. "Look, I've put a chair by the front door, just for you. We'll leave the door wide open. And Rusty is under strict orders to stay right where he is."

"Come see, Daniel! It's beautiful in here," said Amy, stepping into Jane's apartment.

From the hallway Daniel saw a brightly decorated Christmas tree. Beside the tree, wearing a red stocking cap, lay Rusty.

"Aarf!" barked Rusty. He began to get up. Daniel grabbed Jane's arm.

"Stay, Rusty," said Jane sternly. Rusty sat down again, staring mournfully at Daniel.

"He won't bother you, I promise," said Jane. "But you're the boy he's been looking for, you know. He thinks you're his friend."

"*I'll* be his friend," said Amy. "So will Veronica." She ran over to the dog. She patted Rusty's smooth, sleek coat.

Daniel noticed that the dog's ears were down. *Friendly sign number one,* thought Daniel. Slowly he entered the apartment and sat down on the chair near the door. Still, he wasn't crazy about being in the same room with the dog. Nothing had changed. He was just a big baby and always would be! Amy was only five years old, but look at her. *She* wasn't afraid, not one bit. She would love to have a dog like Rusty, more than anything.

"How about some hot chocolate and cookies?" said Jane, passing a big tray.

"Yum," said Amy, choosing a cookie shaped like a Christmas tree.

Jonah chose a candle, and Daniel a chocolate reindeer.

"Now, Rusty," said Jane, taking a cookie from the plate, "you can have a cookie, but first do your stuff. Roll over, please."

Rusty rolled over, then sat up again.

"Give me your paw," said Jane. Rusty put his big paw in her hand, looking very pleased with himself. "Good dog," said Jane.

Rusty barked at her loudly.

"Here you are," said Jane, giving him the cookie. "And now for the best trick of all." Jane picked up her camera from the coffee table. She crossed the room. "I can get Amy, Jonah, and Rusty in the picture from here. Now, smile when I give the signal. And watch Rusty carefully." Jane peered into the camera lens. "Okay, kids. Say pizza!"

"Pizza!" shouted Jonah and Amy.

"Pizza," said Daniel softly.

"Look, Rusty's smiling too!" Amy said.

From across the room Daniel leaned forward to get a better look. Rusty had stretched his mouth so that his teeth were showing!

"Good dog," said Jane, taking the picture. "All right, this is the last cookie," she said to Rusty. "No more."

The dog stared at the rest of the cookies. *Drip. Drip.* His drool made a small puddle on the rug.

"Oh, what a messy dog you are. I'll get some paper towels," said Jane, going into the kitchen.

Daniel began to reach for his mug of hot chocolate. All at once the silver *dreidel* fell from his hand. It bounced two times on the floor. Then it skittered lightly across the room, stopping at Rusty's front paws.

Rusty picked up the *dreidel* in his mouth and stared right at Daniel. Before Daniel knew it, the dog was lumbering across the room, his claws clattering loudly. Heading right toward *him*! Daniel jumped up from his chair.

"Uh-oh," said Amy.

Now Rusty was so close Daniel could see the dog's yellow teeth and the freckles on his wet nose. Daniel stiffened, staring at Rusty. He felt as if he couldn't breathe.

Rusty dropped the *dreidel* at Daniel's feet.

Daniel looked down. *Shin,* said the *dreidel.* Give half.

*Thump. Thump.* Was that his heart pounding? No, it was the dog's tail, thumping the floor like crazy. Friendly sign number two.

Daniel took a deep breath. Slowly he reached for his cookie. His hands shaking

just a little, he gave half of the cookie to
Rusty. The dog's big, rough tongue tickled
his fingers.

"Good dog," whispered Daniel. "Good
dog."

# WEDNESDAY
## A Hanukkah Party to Remember

It was always the same, thought Daniel.
You waited a whole year for Hanukkah.
Then—*poof!* The holiday week was over.

He opened his bedroom window and leaned
out. The snow was coming down hard. Mr.
Rumper was outside, shoveling the walk.

"Merry Christmas, Mr. Rumper," called
Daniel.

"Happy Hanukkah, David!" said Mr.
Rumper with a wave. "They say this snow
will turn to freezing rain by tonight."

"By the way, my name is Daniel," said

Daniel. "Here's a good way to remember. The first part, 'Dan,' rhymes with *'can,' 'fan,' 'man,'* and *'plan.'*"

Mr. Rumper made an "okay" sign with his gloved fingers. "Daniel. Thanks. I'll remember that."

Daniel shut the window and went back to his desk. He was making a new card to go with Amy's Hanukkah gift. Rhymes buzzed in his head. *Bog, cog, fog, frog.*

Jonah came into the bedroom. He flopped down on the bed. "You're not going to believe this," he said.

"Believe what?" Daniel asked absent-mindedly, without looking up. He wrote on Amy's card:

A dog
Is more fun
Than a frog.

"Mom's making orange *latkes* for the party! Dad's making those green ones again. And Mom said they're even thinking of making *purple* ones!" wailed Jonah.

"I know," said Daniel. "But I think carrot and eggplant *latkes* are worth a try. We liked the zucchini ones."

Jonah held his nose. "I can't stand it!"

Something very weird was happening in the Bloom family, thought Daniel. This week Jonah was growing down. Daniel himself was growing up!

He finished the verse on Amy's card:

And you can jog
With a dog.

L _ _ _ ,
↗ Your brother
Daniel
hint: rhymes with 👑

He would help her read it. Underneath the poem, he drew a dog with brownish red fur, sort of like Rusty. There. All done. Now he would go get Amy's gift.

"Where are you going? We have to practice our Hanukkah show," said Jonah, sitting up.

"Again? We've only practiced it a zillion times," Daniel said, pausing at the doorway.

"We need to have a dress rehearsal," said Jonah.

"We'll still have time when I get back," said Daniel.

He tried not to giggle. Jonah was wearing a skirt made from an old bath towel pinned around his waist. He didn't look at all like a Maccabee soldier.

"Real Maccabees wore sandals," Daniel said. "Not sneakers."

"You're right," said Jonah, staring unhappily at his feet. "But my sandals don't fit anymore."

"Neither do mine," said Daniel.

In the kitchen Daniel breathed in the delicious cooking smells. Chicken. Brisket. *Latkes*. Probably hundreds and hundreds of them!

"May I have two of each kind of *latke*?" he asked.

"That's quite a few, don't you think?" said Mrs. Bloom.

"Don't worry. They're not for me. They're a gift." Daniel piled some *latkes* on a plate. He stretched plastic wrap over them. "Do you have some bows I can stick on top?" he asked.

"Sure. Who's the gift for?" his mother asked.

Daniel grinned at her. "For Jane and Rusty."

He went next door and rang the bell. There were turkey smells coming from Jane's apartment. He could hear music and people laughing inside.

"Well, hi!" Jane exclaimed, opening the door.

"Merry Christmas," said Daniel.

Wearing a festive green bow around his neck, Rusty barked happily. He scampered toward Daniel. Nervously Daniel took a few steps backward.

"Whoa, boy!" said Jane, grabbing Rusty's collar firmly.

"These are *latkes*," said Daniel, giving Jane the wrapped plate. "They're for both of you. And I'm wondering if you could give me something in exchange. A dog biscuit."

Daniel described the Hanukkah card he had made for Amy. "I want to tape the dog biscuit inside the card," he said. "Sort of like a promise, you know? I figure we'll be getting our own dog soon. I'm not as scared of Rusty as I used to be. He's only one dog, but it's a start."

Jane nodded. "It's a good start. And there are other friendly dogs like Rusty."

"Zillions, probably," said Daniel.

"Hey," said Jane. "Why don't we take Rusty for a walk?"

"Right now?" asked Daniel.

"Sure. Let's go before the snow gets too deep," said Jane. "You get your coat while I find that dog biscuit."

Rusty gave a little yelp, as if he understood. As if going for a walk with Daniel and Jane was more important than anything.

Outside, the snow was falling quickly and silently. Big Joe Zucchini was now a tall, shapeless mound, still wearing his football helmet.

Jane threw a Frisbee. Rusty leaped to grab it with his teeth, then ran back. His big paws made long tracks in the fresh snow. He dropped the Frisbee at Jane's feet.

"Your turn, Daniel," said Jane.

Daniel threw the Frisbee high and far. Rusty caught it again.

"Good catch!" cried Daniel.

With the Frisbee in his mouth, Rusty raced toward Daniel. Big Joe Zucchini, that great quarterback, was speechless with amazement. Daniel felt brave and scared at

the same time, but the scared feeling was beginning to melt, like snow in the sun.

All afternoon the snow continued to fall. By dusk it had turned to freezing rain. Daniel could hear ice pellets rattling the windowpanes. He looked out the kitchen window. Cars were inching down the street.

"Of course we understand," Mr. Bloom was saying into the kitchen telephone. "There's always next year."

"What's wrong?" asked Mrs. Bloom.

"Aunt Nancy, Uncle Al, and the kids won't be coming tonight," said Mr. Bloom, filling the teakettle with water for tea. "And Aunt Judy's car got stuck in her driveway. I think we'll have to cancel the party. The streets are much too icy for safe driving."

"Oh, phooey!" said Daniel, disappointed. He had really wanted to challenge his cousins to a game of *dreidel*!

"We can still have a party," said Mrs.

Bloom. "It will just be a little smaller, that's all."

After a while the electric teakettle began whistling. Suddenly it stopped in the middle of its song. The kitchen went dark.

"There are no lights in the living room!" said Jonah, running into the kitchen.

"The electricity must be out in the whole apartment," said Mr. Bloom.

"Double phooey," said Daniel. "How can we have a party in the dark?"

Mrs. Bloom rummaged in a drawer for a flashlight and candles. Daniel ran through the darkened apartment to his bedroom. He brought back his own battery-powered radio/flashlight.

*"Freezing rain has snapped power lines all over the city,"* a radio announcer said. *"Many areas are without electricity."*

"Will it be dark for a long, long time?" asked Amy, looking worried.

"I'm sure city employees are working hard to fix things," said Mrs. Bloom with a sigh. "I hope it doesn't take too long. All our food will spoil if we can't refrigerate it."

Daniel stared out the kitchen window. How lonely and strange the city looked now! It was pitch-black outside, except for the cars' headlights. Every now and then a candle or a flashlight's beam lit up an apartment window.

Daniel had an idea.

"Why don't we invite people in the building to come to our party?" he asked.

"Good thinking!" said Jonah, looking at Daniel with admiration. "That means a bigger audience for our Hanukkah show."

Daniel liked the idea of roaming through dark hallways with his emergency flashlight. He would pretend he was on a special mission. "Let's go knock on some doors, guys!" he said to Jonah and Amy.

Mr. Bloom picked up the telephone receiver. "You don't have to do that. The phones are working. Luckily *those* power lines are underground," he said. "Let's see who can come."

The young couple and their baby from the third floor came. So did Mr. and Mrs. Ezra, from down the hall. They brought *latkes,* a big salad, and their menorah. Lara brought her menorah, too. She also brought her parents and grandparents and a big bag of jelly doughnuts, called *sufganiyot.*

Then Mr. Rumper arrived with his two visiting grandsons. Daniel hadn't even known he was a grandfather.

"Hi, Nathaniel," said Mr. Rumper with a wink. "Just kidding. I mean Daniel, of course."

Daniel winked back at him. Maybe Mr. Rumper hadn't remembered his name. But Daniel himself didn't know much about Mr. Rumper, either. Except that he was good at shoveling walks.

Soon Jane arrived. She was carrying a turkey on a platter and had her camera around her neck. With her were three friends, her brother, her aunt, and her parents.

And Rusty. "Arrf!" he barked, scampering to Daniel. Daniel leaned down to scratch behind Rusty's ear.

"Well," said Mr. Bloom softly, "look at that."

"Daniel!" exclaimed Amy.

Daniel grinned at his sister. She was going to love his little present. In a million, zillion years he couldn't have thought of a better one.

"Welcome, everybody," said Mrs. Bloom. "Come and gather around. Let's light all these menorahs!"

All the candles on all the menorahs were lit and the blessing sung. The glow lit up the room. Shadows danced on the walls.

"Oh, how lovely," said Jane, snapping a picture.

"Please take your seats, everyone," said Daniel. "It's time for our Hanukkah show."

Jonah stepped forward and began.

*"The Hanukkah lights are not to keep*
  *you warm,*

*They are not to bring light when there's*
   *a very bad storm,*
*They don't do any work as they shine so*
   *bright,*
*They just remind us of the wonders of*
   *another night."*

"And now, ladies and gentlemen," said Daniel. "We bring you the candle that does all the work—the *Shammes* Candle!"

Amy stepped forward. Her red hair glowed in the candlelight.

"I light the candles from left to right," Amy began. She held up her right arm, then her left.

"Left arm first," whispered Daniel.

"I light the candles from left to right," repeated Amy, holding up her left arm first, then her right. "Every single Hanukkah night!"

Amy bowed. Everyone clapped and Rusty barked. Jane snapped a picture.

Jonah came forward again. "We now bring you the Two Maccabee Brothers!"

Jonah stepped backward into the shadows. He came forward again, with Daniel at his side. Jonah began:

*"We will tell you a story and you will say,*
*'What a wonderful story you've told us*
*today!'*
*Does the name 'Antiochus' ring a bell?*
*Well, he's part of the story we will now*
*tell!"*

And Daniel continued:

*"It's the Hanukkah tale, it's not too long,*
*About a troop of fighters, brave and*
*strong,*
*Mattathias and Judah, all the Maccabees*
*loyal,*
*And the rededication of the temple with*
*the miracle oil."*

Then Jonah and Daniel took turns reading the story from *The Happy Hanukkah Holiday Book*. Daniel gazed at the audience as Jonah read. So what if he and Jonah and Amy were wearing bath towels and sneakers? You couldn't really tell by candlelight. A sudden shiver went up and down his spine.

*This is just how it was in the days of the Maccabees!* he thought. No electricity. No TV. No radios or computers. Just family and friends, singing and praying and telling stories together. Helping each other feel brave when the night was dark and cold. Or when their enemies came.

And so what if he and Jonah hadn't had time to figure out the whole Hanukkah story in rhyme?

*Shiver.*

Wasn't it a miracle that they were still telling the story, thousands of years later?

Daniel and Jonah bowed deeply. Rusty barked as the audience clapped. Jane snapped another picture.

"Bravo!" called Mr. Rumper.

Mr. and Mrs. Bloom began carrying out platters of food.

"Just one more picture before we sit down to eat," said Jane. "Gather 'round, everybody!"

"Too bad they didn't have cameras in ancient times," said Jonah. "Somebody could have taken photos of that eight-day miracle oil to prove it really happened."

Jane focused the camera. "Say pizza!" she said.

*"Pizza!"* everyone shouted.

"Zucchini!" said Daniel joyfully.

And Rusty smiled.

That night Daniel dreamt about the Maccabee again. The two of them swapped stories under an olive tree.

"Well, I've got to go now," said the Maccabee-in-the-dream. He did two deep-knee bends, then retied his sandals. "Wish me good *L-U-C-K*."

"Good luck," said Daniel-in-the-dream. "It was great to meet you."

"Great to meet you, too," said the Maccabee. "Tell me, does this story turn out all right in the end?"

"Well, yes," said Daniel, happy to share what he knew.

"Oh, good!" said the Maccabee, looking relieved. He stood straight and tall. "Actually, I'm not that surprised." He patted a little cloth purse hanging from his belt. "Got my peanuts for the elephants right here. Thanks for the idea."

"Before you go," said Daniel, "let me tell you my new peanut plan."

# latke recipes

## POTATO LATKES

*Ask an adult to help you with this recipe. It requires grating by hand (or the use of a food processor if you have one) as well as frying in hot oil.*

> 4  potatoes, peeled
> 1  large onion
> 3  eggs
> ¼  cup flour
> 1  teaspoon salt
> freshly ground black pepper
> pinch of baking soda
> vegetable oil
> sour cream and applesauce

1. Grate the potatoes by hand or in a food processor, then grate the onion.
2. Insert the steel blade in the processor and add the eggs, flour, salt, pepper, and soda. Pulse just until mixed. (If you do not own a food processor, add the eggs, flour, salt, pepper, and soda by hand and mix well.)

3. In a large skillet, heat ¼ inch of oil. The oil must be very hot. (You can use two skillets and fry two batches at once, for speed!)

4. Spoon large tablespoonfuls of potato batter into the hot oil, flattening with the back of the spoon. Brown, turning *only once.*

5. Drain on paper towels. (You can keep the *latkes* in a warm oven as you fry the remaining batter.)

6. Serve with sour cream and applesauce.

*Makes 2½ to 3 dozen latkes.*


*Two Make-Ahead Tips*

• You can prepare the batter a few hours ahead, cover with a thin layer of flour, and refrigerate. Remove the flour with a spoon before frying.

• You can freeze *latkes.* They'll still taste wonderful, though not extraordinary.


*This recipe by Joanne Rocklin has previously appeared in* Writers in the Kitchen, *compiled by Tricia Gardella, Boyds Mills Press, Honesdale, Pennsylvania, 1998.*

# MIRACLE ZUCCHINI LATKES
### (they use hardly any oil!)

*Ask an adult to help you with this recipe. It requires grating by hand (or the use of a food processor if you have one) as well as baking in a hot oven.*

5  *medium zucchini, unpeeled*
3  *scallions, sliced*
2  *eggs*
²/₃ *cup seasoned bread crumbs (or more if needed, up to 1 cup)*
*salt and pepper to taste*
*vegetable oil*

1. Preheat the oven to 425 degrees.
2. Clean the zucchini well. Grate by hand or in batches in a food processor. Lay out the zucchini on layers of ink-free paper towels; cover with more paper towels. Let stand for half an hour.
3. Place the zucchini in a bowl and mix with the other ingredients (except the oil). Use your hands to make a "dough" that sticks together.
4. Pour about 1 tablespoon of oil on each cookie sheet (you will need two sheets). Spread the oil with a paper towel.

5. Mound the zucchini mixture on the cookie sheets with a tablespoon. Press down with a fork to make pancakes about 2½ inches wide.

6. Bake for about 12 minutes, or until the pancakes turn brown on the bottom (not the top). Turn the pancakes over and bake for an additional 5 minutes.

*Makes 18 to 20 small latkes.*

*From* Melting Pot Memories, *by Judy Kancigor, G & R Publishing Co., Waverly, Iowa, 1999.*

## About the Author

JOANNE ROCKLIN is the acclaimed author of more than a dozen books for children. A former elementary-school teacher and psychologist, she now writes full-time. She is a member of the Advisory Committee for the Museum of Tolerance "Once Upon a World" Storytelling Program of the Simon Wiesenthal Center in Los Angeles and is a founding member of the outreach organization California Readers. Originally from Montreal, Joanne Rocklin has two grown sons and lives in Los Angeles with her husband, Gerry, and three cats.

## About the Illustrator

CATHARINE O'NEILL, who has illustrated numerous picture books and children's novels, lives in Ithaca, New York, with her partner, daughter, and dogs.